T0145274

TIM QUINCY
The Elevator Kid

Rhudenia Hopes-Johnson

Tim Quincy
THE ELEVATOR KID

Copyright © 2018 Rhudenia Hopes-Johnson.

All rights reserved. No part of this book may be used or reproduced by any means, graphic, electronic, or mechanical, including photocopying, recording, taping or by any information storage retrieval system without the written permission of the author except in the case of brief quotations embodied in critical articles and reviews.

iUniverse books may be ordered through booksellers or by contacting:

iUniverse
1663 Liberty Drive
Bloomington, IN 47403
www.iuniverse.com
1-800-Authors (1-800-288-4677)

Because of the dynamic nature of the Internet, any web addresses or links contained in this book may have changed since publication and may no longer be valid. The views expressed in this work are solely those of the author and do not necessarily reflect the views of the publisher, and the publisher hereby disclaims any responsibility for them.

Any people depicted in stock imagery provided by Getty Images are models, and such images are being used for illustrative purposes only.
Certain stock imagery © Getty Images.

ISBN: 978-1-5320-5326-9 (sc)
ISBN: 978-1-5320-5327-6 (e)

Library of Congress Control Number: 2018908101

Print information available on the last page.

iUniverse rev. date: 08/07/2018

Meet Tim Quincy, The Elevator Kid. He is 9 years old.

His bedroom has an amazing view of the Houston skyline because he lives in the JP Morgan Chase Tower.

He has 30 red cars and 50 yellow school buses carefully lined up along the windowsill overlooking the city.

He loves this skyscraper because it has 75 floors and offers the best view of the city's skyline.

But his favorite part of the building is the Otis Elevator.

"Hey mom, can I please ride in the glass elevators to the Observation Deck?" Tim asks. He loves to visit the 60th floor Observation Deck every chance he gets.

"I have to cook our Sunday dinner. I can't take you now. I am sorry."

Tim thinks really, really hard and gets an idea.

"What if I go by myself? I am a big boy and know what buttons to push."

"I don't know."

"I just love the wide glass planes and tall ceilings in the Otis Elevator" he insists. Tim's mother heart is softened because she knows how much he loves elevators.

She agrees that he can go by himself as long as he make it home in time for dinner, which makes him feel very proud and grown up. Thanks mom. You're welcome sweetie.

Tim steps into the elevator as he has many times before with his mother. But alone in the elevator, the keypad looks different. He looks for the 60th floor, but instead of numbers, the buttons have his favorite buildings on them.

"Wow! I am in a magical elevator!" he exclaims.

He chooses the button with the One World Trade building in NYC, closes his eyes, and pushes it.

Ding!

The elevator doors glide open, and Tim sees the view across the Brooklyn Bridge, Statue of Liberty in view. Two children, Akirah and Seth are playing a game of Chess at the corner table of their home, and they look at him incredulously.

"Wow! You live in 1 Trade Center! Did you know that it only takes one minute for this Otis elevator to climb from the lobby to the 100th floor in the Freedom Tower?" Tim asks.

"No," says the Seth, "but this is the coolest building in NYC!"

"I agree. Do you know how many elevators are inside this building?" Tim asks.

"No, we've never counted them." Akirah states.

"There are 71 elevators! And five express elevators."

"How do you know all that?" they ask.

"I know because I am Tim, the Elevator Kid."

"Nice to meet you." My name is Seth and this is my Sister Akirah.

"Wow, that's amazing!" Akirah says.

"Would you like to ride in my magic elevator?"

"I don't know if we should" states Seth.

"Can we go to the Eiffel Tower?" Akirah asks.

"Absolutely!" Tim says.

Bonjour! My Name is Marcellus.

"It's even better than I thought it would be!" Akirah exclaims.

"I know! The two Otis Duo-Lift elevators in the Eiffel tower travel up to 500 feet-per-minute," Tim adds.

"How do you know that?" Marcellus asks. He has been to the Eiffel Tower many times and never thought about the elevators even once.

"I am Tim, The Elevator Kid, and guess what else? These elevators carry up to 40 passengers up and down, simultaneously." "What does that mean?" Asks Seth. "They move at the same time, like your hands you can bring the right up as the left goes down."

"That makes sense" Akirah says.

"Would you like to use my binoculars?" Marcellus offers.

"Thank you!" she says. Marcellus points out the Sacre Coeur and Notre Dame Cathedrals, the Arc of Triumph, The Obelisk, and the Thames River.

"Thank you for sharing your city with us" Seth hands back the binoculars to Marcellus.

"Would you like to bring your binoculars and see some more amazing places?" Tim asks Marcellus.

"Yes, but how?"

"We didn't get here in an ordinary elevator. You have to try to it believe it."

"I've always wanted to go to the Tokyo Skytree" Marcellus says.

"Let's go!" says Tim.

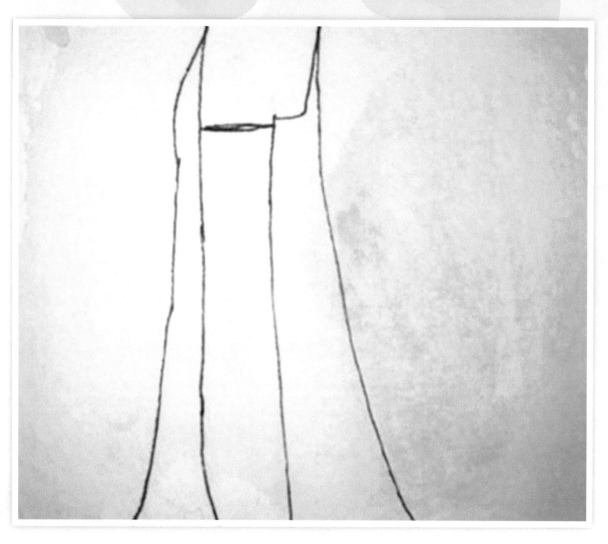

"Is this real?" Marcellus asks.

"Can we walk on the glass?" Akirah asks.

"It's okay, everyone. The glass skywalk leads to a glass platform. Let's check it out!" Tim says.

The children hold tight to the arm rails and gingerly walk across the glass.

"This is a very safe building meant to withstand earthquakes" Tim says.

"How is that possible?" Akirah asks. "There's a system of reinforced concrete that keeps the building's

system of gravity in the base." Tim answers.

"Like if I fall into you, you might not fall, but if your feet are firmly planted, your upper body can shift and stay upright," Hello Nori says, turning to the group of children.

"That makes sense."

"Hey, I can see Mt. Fuji right" Marcellus exclaims, pointing his finger and looking through his binoculars.

"I can show you a cooler view than that" says Nori. She takes them to the Upper Platform and says, "Look below."

"The people are like ants!" Seth cries. Through the glass floor, the children can see all the way down all 35 floors to the street below.

"Those real cars look like my toy cars!" Tim says and feels a little homesick.

"Are you on a school trip?" the Japanese girl asks.

"No, I am Tim, the Elevator Kid, and we are using my magic elevator to travel."

"That's amazing. I've always wanted to visit the Burkjhalifa Tower." She says.

"Me, too!" Tim says. "Let's go."

"I can't believe it!" Akira whispers, holding Nori hand.

"We're in the tallest building in the world" Nori whispers back. They step out of the glass elevators through the stainless-steel doors.

"This building has the world's fastest double-decker elevators," Tim says as the children look through the glass in wonder. A boy in a kaftan notices the group.

"How are they double?" Marcellus asks Tim.

"They stop on two floors at once" . Ahmad answers.

"Did you also know that the Burkjkhalifa also has the tallest elevator in the world?" Tim asks him.

"Yes, all 124 floors!" . Ahmad says proudly.

"That's three times as tall as the Eiffel Tower" Marcellus says in amazement.

"We can't see the ground this time" Akirah says, looking out into the clouds.

"This is also the tallest building in the world" the Japanese Girl shares.

"There's no building in the world with a taller or faster elevator" . Ahmad brags.

"This is not the only cool building in the world" Seth replies. "I live in 1 Trade Center, and we have 71 elevators in total."

"This building only has 68," Tim says.

"How do you know so many things about the Burkjkhalifa?" . Ahmad asks.

"He's Tim, the Elevator Kid!" Akira answers for him. "He has a magic elevator and has been taking us all over the world."

"Can you go to the Al Noor Tower?" . Ahmad asks.

"It hasn't been built yet" Nori protests,

"Don't forget that my elevator is magic, it's worth a shot," Tim says.

"This is the most beautiful I have ever seen!" Akirah says, running her hand along the gold railing.

"I want to live in this elevator. It's better than my bedroom" Nori says.

The children exit the elevator in wonder that they are inside a building that only exists in the minds of its architects.

"What's so special here?" Seth grumbles.

"Al Noor Tower is special because it stands 540 meters tall and have 54 single-deck elevators representing all 54 countries of Africa" Tim says.

"It will be the tallest building in Africa when it's finished". Ahmad includes.

"The name means 'Tower of Light'" says Akirah.

"How do you know that?" Ahmad asks.

"My mother is from Morocco, even though I am American."

"There are no kids here" Seth says with disappointment.

"They aren't here yet because the building isn't really here. Even my magic elevator has its limits."

"Well, I think it's extraordinary" Marcellus says. He is looking through his binoculars. "Look at the city skyline!" The children marvel at the tall, square-shaped tower in the distance.

"What's that?" asks the Nori.

"It looks like a cathedral steeple" says Marcellus.

"You're close, it's the Hassan II, the tallest mosque in the world" says Ahmad.

"Would you like to see some Christian architecture?" Tim asks.

"Sacre Coeur?" Marcellus asks.

"This one has amazing Otis elevators."

"Where?" Seth, curiosity getting the best of him.

"Rio di Janero!" Tim answers.

"Welcome to the first-ever Otis Gen2 elevator. It was designed to run without lubrication so there's no chance of a spill in the park," Tim says.

"What a beautiful park!" Akirah says, pointing town the mountain.

"It's the largest urban garden in the world," Nai says, joining the group.

"The Otis Gen2 is also 40% more energy efficient than other elevators," Tim says.

"What a great company!" Marcellus replies, and Tim grins from ear-to-ear because his new friend understands his hobby.

"We can see the whole city from here! Ahmad says.

"Cool, we're standing near the statue's arm," Seth adds, "I can almost touch it."

"Don't lean too far," Akirah cautions her brother.

"I feel so big in the Skytree, but here I feel so small," Marcellus says, looking up at the statue's face.

"Check out the other side! There's water, Ahmad signals the children to the other side of the observation deck.

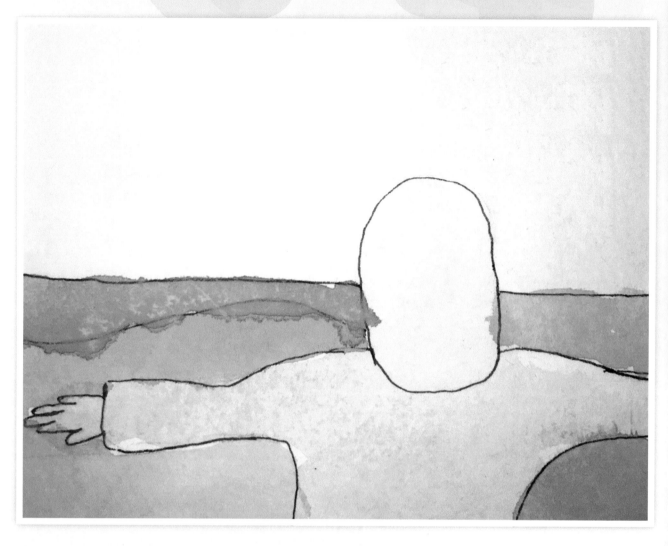

They join him and see the vast, sparking water of the South Atlantic Ocean.

"Want to use my binoculars?" Marcellus asks, handing them to Akirah.

"Is this your first time in Brazil?" Nai asks the group.

"Yes, we're with Tim, the Elevator Kid," Seth answers.

"Would you like to join us?" Nori asks her.

"That depends. Where are you going next?"

"Let's go back to America. I want to show you the world's fastest elevator," Tim says. "Guess where it is."

"Not Dubai," Ahmad pauses. "London?"

"Washington D.C.?" asks Marcellus.

"Wait and see!" he says, and they pile into the elevator.

The elevator doors open, and the children are in the John Hancock Centre in Chicago, IL.

"We're on the 94th floor!" Tim announces as the children step out of the elevator.

"So, how fast are these elevators?" Ahmad asks.

"These Otis elevators travel at 549 meters/minute or 20 miles per hour," Tim replies.

"Look! There's the Sears Tower. It used to be the tallest building in the world," Marcellus says, pointing to the building.

"Now it's a normal size" Nori says with disappointment.

"This city is so much bigger than Rio!" Nai exclaims.

"Do you watch baseball?" Nori asks. "There's Wrigley field!"

"Take a look through my binoculars" Marcellus offers.

"Is that the Centennial Ferris wheel?" Seth asks, pointing.

"Yes, it is," says Tim.

"The Ferris wheel makes me think of waffles with sugar" says Marcellus.

"It makes me think of funnel cake," says Akirah.

"I'm hungry," says the Nori and Ahmad.

"at any of these places we visited," Ahmad says, rubbing his belly. It begins to grumble.

"Hey, would you all like to come to Sunday dinner with my family?" Tim asks.

"Will they mind that we're a little—" Nai gestures, trying to find the word.

"Different?" Marcellus fills in for her.

"We have visitors all the time, plus, I can show you the view from Houston's Chase Tower."

"Let's do it!"

The elevator doors open, and the children hear laughter from the family. They look up to see Tim and his friends and go silent.

"Tim, we have been worried! Where have you been?" his mother asks. Tim tries to open his mouth, but no words come out. He gestures to his assortment of friends.

"I didn't know you were bringing friends, let's get some extra chairs. Welcome!" she says to them. Tim's brother helps the children find chairs and sit with the family.

"Thank you, Ma'am," says Akirah.

"Tim is the coolest kid ever!" Ahmad tells her.

"Yeah, the coolest elevator kid," Marcellus adds, and she beams.

"What did you see on the observation deck?" she asks.

"You wouldn't believe me if I told you," Tim says, and all the children smile at each other, heaping their plates with Fried Fish, Bowl of Crawfish Etouffee, Mac and Cheese, Green Beans, Spinach Strawberry Pecan Salad, French Bread,Green Beans, "Lipton Rasberry Tea with Gingerale" and his mother's best Peach Cobbler and Chocolate chip Cookies for dessert.

Tim thinks about his 30 red cars and 50 yellow school buses all lined on his windowsill and decides that he still lives in the best building with the best elevators, ever.

THE END

This is for "Quincy Jr., Aaron, and Braylon my inspiration" … Special acknowledgements Cindy Childress PhD, Jada Washington the Best Illustrator keep reaching for the stars! To her mother Charlette Washington, Morganshortgraphics, *My dearest friends and family who are my biggest Supporters, for the countless hours you gave me your listening ear about my book I love you Fred Jr., Tina, DK, Zenobia B., Geraldine, Stacy, Thanks my Bro. Louis A. for the advise on editors, Quincy Sr. Seed Capital, Polk for marketing strategies*, to my parents Fred and Melva, Brother Aunties Rita, Verna and Veronica., Uncle Melvern r.i.p. Co-Workers Robin, Ms. Jackson, Ms.Turner, Mr. Holmes, Rita U. r.i.p, Leola, Marc & Marcie, Gloria, Kim G., Dawnece, Hopes, Williams,Taylor, and Johnson family. Last not least all the Beautiful Amazing children on the Autism Spectrum this is for you!

Printed in the United States
By Bookmasters